W9-BVK-255

WITHDRAWN FROM
COLLECTION

THE BUFFALO SOLDIER

By Sherry Garland
Illustrated by
Ronald Himler

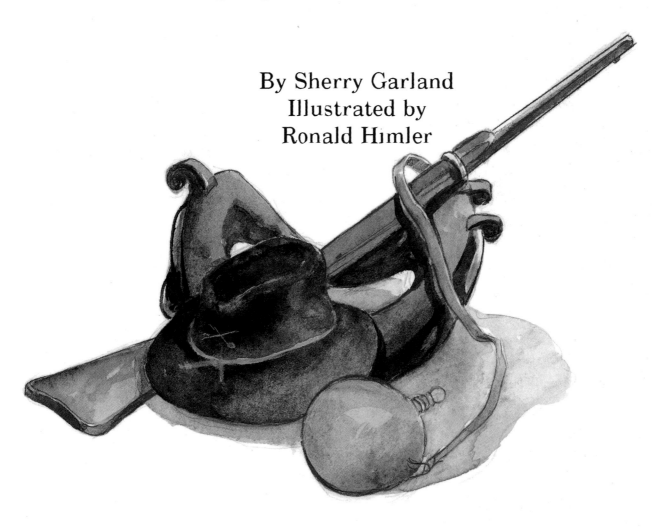

MANDAN PUBLIC LIBRARY

PELICAN PUBLISHING COMPANY
Gretna 2006

Acknowledgments
I would like to thank the staff of Fort Davis National Historic Site and Fort Concho
National Historic Landmark for sharing their expertise and answering my hundreds of
questions. And I offer a special thank-you to Paul Matthews, of the Buffalo Soldiers
National Museum in Houston, Texas.

Text copyright © 2006
By Sherry Garland

Illustrations copyright © 2006
By Ronald Himler
All rights reserved

*The word "Pelican" and the depiction of a pelican are
trademarks of Pelican Publishing Company, Inc.,
and are registered in the U.S. Patent and Trademark Office.*

Library of Congress Cataloging-in-Publication Data

Garland, Sherry.
  The buffalo soldier / by Sherry Garland ; illustrated by Ronald Himler.
     p. cm.
  Summary: Realizing that his future lies in owning land, not just being free, a young
man raised as a slave becomes a buffalo soldier—a member of an all-black cavalry
regiment formed to protect white settlers from Indians, bandits, and outlaws, and
that later fought in the Spanish-American War. Includes historical note.
  Includes bibliographical references.
  ISBN-13: 978-1-58980-391-6 (hardcover : alk. paper)
 1. United States. Army. Cavalry, 10th—History—Juvenile fiction. 2. United States.
Army—African American troops—Juvenile fiction. 3. African American soldiers—
Juvenile fiction. [1. United States. Army.—African American troops—Fiction. 2.
United States. Army. Cavalry, 10th—Fiction. 3. African Americans—Fiction. 4.
Soldiers—Fiction. 5. West (U.S.)—History—1860-1890—Fiction.] I. Himler, Ronald,
ill. II. Title.
  PZ7.G18415Buf 2006
  [Fic]—dc22
                                200601248

Printed in Singapore
Published by Pelican Publishing Company, Inc.
1000 Burmaster Street, Gretna, Louisiana 70053

Author's Note

Since the American Revolution, African-Americans have shown their ability as soldiers. More than 180,000 fought for the Union during the Civil War, yet they had not been allowed to join the U.S. Army as regulars. Instead, they were placed in "colored volunteer" units.

This changed in 1866 when Congress passed a law that ordered the creation of six black regiments in the regular army—the Ninth and Tenth Cavalry and the Thirty-eighth through Forty-first Infantry regiments. Three years later, the four infantry units were combined to form the Twenty-fourth and Twenty-fifth Infantry.

The men who joined these regiments were single men from all occupations, with the majority being farmers. Many were former slaves. They joined the army to escape dire poverty, earn a steady income, gain respect, get away from a past of slavery, and receive an education. The majority could not read or write because of laws in slave states that forbade it. As enlisted men, they could not become high-ranking officers. Their commanders were always white, but many of the tough, experienced sergeants were black.

The new black regiments were immediately transported to the Western frontier of the United States to occupy military forts in Kansas, Indian Territory, and Texas. They later served in New Mexico, Arizona, the mountain states, and the Great Plains states. Their duties were to protect settlers from hostile Indians, rustlers, outlaws like Billy the Kid, and Mexican banditos. They guarded mail routes, helped build forts and roads, assisted in mapping uncharted areas, oversaw distribution of food on some Indian reservations, and protected telegraph and railroad crews. In fact, one-fifth of the U.S. Cavalry was African-American at that time.

During one of their earliest skirmishes with Indians, the troopers of the Tenth Cavalry were dubbed "buffalo soldiers" by the Cheyenne, probably because of the similarity between the soldiers' curly hair and the curly hair on the head of the buffalo, but also because of their tenacity and bravery, two characteristics of the buffalo long admired by the Plains Indians. The nickname soon spread to the Ninth Cavalry, then to the black infantry regiments. As time passed, the name would be applied to all black regiments.

The buffalo soldiers faced many hardships during the Indian Wars of 1866-90, from freezing blizzards on the Great Plains to blistering desert heat in the rugged Southwest. They often were given inferior horses and supplies and the most undesirable assignments. They sometimes faced harsh racial prejudice from local residents, but the black soldiers time and again displayed their courage and loyalty. The black regiments had the lowest desertion rates of any. Eighteen buffalo soldiers won the Congressional Medal of Honor during the Indian Wars.

In 1898, buffalo soldiers charged up San Juan Hill in Cuba during the Spanish-American War, and they later served in the Philippines, Hawaii, and Mexico. They continued to serve in the U.S. Army through all American wars. During the Korean War (1950-53), the "buffalo soldier" regiments were officially dissolved. At that time, segregation in the army was done away with, and black soldiers fought alongside American soldiers of all colors and origins.

The news come on a hot, dusty day in June,
eighteen hundred and sixty-five.
Word spread like prairie fire from the Big House,
through the Quarters, down to the bottom fields
where Mama and us was chopping cotton.

Ol' Master, he look pale as a ghost
when he ride up and say,
"The cruel war is over at last.
You'll be my slaves no more."

Sister, she shout and sing the jubilee;
but Mama, she fall down on her knees and cry.

Seems like this being freedmen's
not what it's cracked up to be.
One day Mama up and says,
"We still got no land, got no money.
What we got is plenty of sweat and toil,
plowing 'nother man's fields, picking 'nother man's cotton."

So I walk to New Orleans and put my *X* on the line
when I hear tell the U.S. Army is looking for young Negro men
to serve on the Western frontier.
They promise to pay me thirteen dollars a month.
More money than that I never saw at once.
Surely a man can save it up
and buy a piece of land to call his own.

The army put me in a cavalry regiment,
but Lordy I never rode a horse before.
From the looks of the dirt on their britches,
neither did most of the other new recruits.
Some of them fought for the Union
in the Civil War not long past,
and have that tired look in their eyes.

My sergeant, he's mean as a skunk
and drills us through the day.
Must be a hundred times I hear him holler,
"Troopers, you got to train harder than the rest
'cause all the nation is watching you."

A soldier lives, works, and dies by the bugle.
We get up at dawn to the sound of reveille
and muster for roll call and inspection.
Then we tend the horses.
Those animals get to eat before we do.
We got drills and more drills and work details—
cutting stones, laying bricks,
putting up new buildings everywhere.

'Round five o'clock, we welcome the sound of retreat,
then round 'bout six the call to the mess hall.
It's mostly beans and pork and bread,
maybe a little beef, or a sweet roastin' ear.

We just get a little time to ourselves
before the bugle sounds tattoo
and we all repair to the barracks
to our lumpy mattresses stuffed with hay.

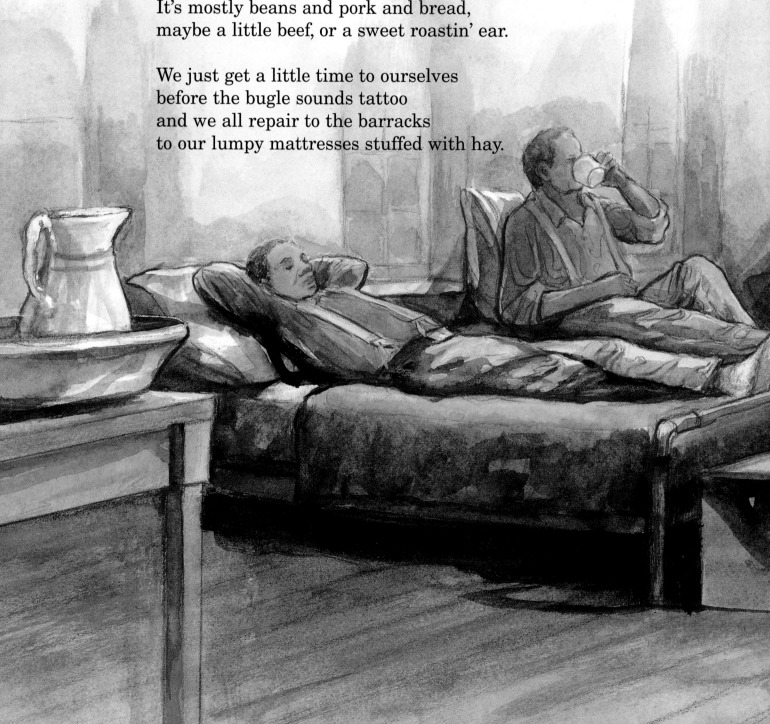

Of an evening, whenever I get a chance,
I go to school on the post.
The chaplain teaches us to read and write
and tells us about American history, too.
I attend in the same room
where the white officers' children
get their learning during the day.

MANDAN PUBLIC LIBRARY

Captain says if I learn to read and write,
maybe someday I'll get promoted to sergeant,
as far as an enlisted man can get up the line.

Just imagine what Ol' Master would say if he saw me now.
Maybe I'll write him a letter to let him know
I'm making something of myself.

Every week we escort somebody—
supply wagons full of goods, wagon trains of families
moving west to find their dreams,
or mail coaches running to El Paso.

It's a most common sight to see the soldiers
racing down the road alongside a coach,
horses at full gallop and guns blazing
at the bandits not far behind.

When the Comanche moon is high in September,
Indians come from out of nowhere,
striking fast as lightning, then scattering to the wind.

We go on patrols looking for their raiding parties
who've left the reservations where they were put.

The buffalo herds are mighty thin now,
killed by buffalo runners who shot them down,
took their hides, and left the carcasses to rot in the sun.
"Three million killed in two years' time," I heard tell.
When I think of all the hungry Indians on the reserves
who have hardly any meat at all,
can't blame them for running off now and again.

Sometimes it gets powerful lonely
when we're camped out under the stars.
I think about Mama and all the folks back home.
Wonder if it's worth the trouble
staying in the army another hitch.
But when I think about being in rags and hungry, too,
guess it's not so bad after all.

From time to time we protect the telegraph crew,
and even help them set the poles and string the lines.

We help the railroad surveyors find their way around.

One year we covered more than a thousand miles
mapping every river and creek and spring
in this desolate and rugged no man's land.
We went up mountains and down canyons
to places where only cactus and rattlesnakes live.
But I didn't mind the work,
for it was better than doing drills.

The paymaster wagon rolls in 'bout every two months
in a cloud of dust, escorted by soldiers in blue.
We are in the highest spirits you ever saw.

Some of the men squander their pay on foolishness
in the nearby town, where saloons
and gambling parlors burst at the seams.
My friend spends his money on fancy goods
from the post trader's store—
a gold watch chain, a bright bow tie or straw hat,
a plug of chewing tobacco, tins of tasty food.

But I have better things to do with my hard-earned pay.

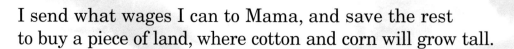

I send what wages I can to Mama, and save the rest
to buy a piece of land, where cotton and corn will grow tall.

Got my eye on a pretty washerwoman named Sally
who works on Suds Row and I know she likes me, too.
We plan to marry come June.
Can't wait to move out of the barracks,
where the smell of stinky feet
and dirty boots won't be missed one bit.

Holidays are something special 'round here—
no work or drills all day long!
The officers' wives throw a fine celebration.
They deck out the main hall and set up tables of food.
Soldiers have footraces, boxing, and baseball.

But best of all is the regimental band.
They play music so sweet and good
it makes your feet want to do a jig.
The officers and their wives look grand
in their fancy clothes and high-button shoes
dancing waltzes and quadrilles.

Me and Sally know a good dance or two ourselves.

Time is marching on and taking me with it.
Served in forts from Kansas to Texas to Arizona
and now to this cold land of the Sioux.
Had children born here, there, and in between.

Spent time fighting Apache and Comanche,
Kiowa and Cheyenne, Shoshone and Crow,
Arapaho and Lakota, Kickapoo and Lipan.
Chased warriors like Victorio and Geronimo
and followers of old gray-haired Sitting Bull.

Sally says she hopes my fingers freeze off
so I can't sign up for five more years.

Been in the army for thirty years.
I'm proud to say that I now wear
first sergeant's stripes on my sleeves.

When the Indian Wars ended back in 1890,
thought I'd seen all the fighting I would ever see,
but now here we are getting ready
to charge up San Juan Hill to help out
Teddy Roosevelt's Rough Riders
in this Spanish-American War.

I promised Sally if I live through this,
I'll leave the army for good.
And this time I mean it!

Well, sir, here I am, an old man, stooped and bent.

That fertile valley below is where herds of buffalo
once shook the ground;
where the Comanche and Kiowa
once whooped and hollered wild and free;
where cowboys once drove longhorns
up miles and miles of trail.
They're gone now, one and all,
and a highway splits the hills.

Yesterday I got a letter from my grandson
who is fighting in this Second World War.
He said the army wants to disband the cavalry
and do away with horses for good.
Now that's a shame, seeing as how a man
can't talk to his Jeep on a lonely winter night.

My grandson was complaining 'bout the food,
'bout the saddle soreness and the loneliness,
'bout his sergeant who's mean as a skunk.

I just have to smile, and nod my head.
You see, once I was a soldier, too.

Selected Bibliography

Cobblestone 16, no. 2 (February 1995).

Cox, Clinton. *The Forgotten Heroes: The Story of the Buffalo Soldiers.* New York: Scholastic, 1993.

Dobak, William A., and Thomas D. Phillips. *The Black Regulars 1866-1898.* Norman: University of Oklahoma Press, 2001.

Fowler, Arlen L. *The Black Infantry in the West, 1869-1891.* Norman: University of Oklahoma Press, 1996.

Langellier, John P. *Men A-Marching: The African-American Soldier in the West, 1866-1896.* Springfield, Pa.: Steven Wright, 1995.

Leckie, William H. *The Buffalo Soldiers: A Narrative of the Negro Cavalry in the West.* Norman: University of Oklahoma Press, 1967.

Nankivell, John H. *Buffalo Soldier Regiment: History of the Twenty-fifth United States Infantry, 1869-1926.* Lincoln: University of Nebraska Press, 2001.

Utley, Robert M. *Fort Davis National Historic Site, Texas.* National Park Service Handbook Series, no. 38. Washington, D.C., 1965.

Wooster, Robert. *Fort Davis: Outpost on the Texas Frontier.* Fred Rider Cotten Popular History Series, no. 8. Austin: Texas State Historical Association, 1994.